The Missing Coach

Thomas the Tank Engine & Friends

A BRITT ALLCROFT COMPANY PRODUCTION

Based on The Railway Series by The Rev W Awdry
© Gullane (Thomas) LLC 2002

Visit the Thomas & Friends web site at www.thomasthetankengine.com

ISBN 0-439-33854-9

12 11 10 9 8 7 6 5 4 3 2 1   2 3 4 5 6 7/0
Printed in the U.S.A.
First Scholastic printing, August 2002

This edition is available for distribution only through the direct-to-home market.

The Missing Coach

by
The REV. W. AWDRY

SCHOLASTIC INC.

New York   Toronto   London   Auckland   Sydney
Mexico City   New Delhi   Hong Kong   Buenos Aires

Some workmen came to give the twins their numbers. Donald was 9 and Douglas 10. When the men went away, they were left alone in the Shed.

"Ye may have noticed, Douggie, that those painters forgot somethin'."

"What did they forget?"

"They painted brand new numbers on our tenders, but they put none on us." Donald winked broadly at his twin. "Ye mean," grinned Douglas, "that we can . . ."

"Just that," chuckled Donald. "Keep it down. Here's the Inspector."

"Now 9 and 10," smiled the Inspector, "here's Duck. He'll show you around before you start work."

The twins enjoyed themselves, and were soon friends with Duck. They didn't mind what they did. They tackled goods trains and coaches easily; for, once the twins had shunted them, freight cars knew better than to try any tricks.

"We like it fine here," said Donald.

"That's good," smiled Duck, "but take my tip, watch out for Gordon, Henry, and James. They're sure to try some nonsense!"

"Don't worry yourself," chuckled Douglas. "We'll soon settle them."

Donald and Douglas had deep-toned whistles.

"They sound like buses," said Gordon.

"Or ships," sniggered Henry.

"Tug-boat Annie!" laughed Gordon. "Ha! Ha!"

Donald and Douglas cruised quietly up, one on each side.
"Ye wouldn't be making fun of us would ye now?" asked Donald.

Gordon and Henry jumped. They glanced nervously from
side to side.

"Er, no," said Gordon.

"No, no, certainly not," said Henry.

"That's fine," said Douglas. "Now just mind the both of ye,
and keep it that way."

That was the way Gordon and Henry kept it!

Every day, punctually at 3:30, Gordon steams in with the express. It is called THE WILD NOR' WESTER, and is full of people from England, Wales, and Scotland. There is also a special coach for passengers traveling to places on Thomas' Branch Line.

When the other coaches are taken away empty, engines have to remember to shunt the special coach to the Bay platform. It does not wait there long. Thomas, with Annie and Clarabel, comes hurrying from the junction to fetch it. Thomas is very proud of his special coach.

One afternoon Douglas helped Duck in the yard while Donald waited to take a goods train to the other end of the line. As Duck was busy arranging Donald's freight cars, Douglas offered to take away Gordon's coaches.

Douglas was enjoying himself, when an awful thought struck him. "I hope Sir Topham Hatt doesn't find out I shouldn't be here. I couldn't handle going back." He worried so much over this that he forgot about Thomas' special coach.

He pushed it with the others into the carriage siding, then ambled along to join Donald at the water column. As he went, Thomas scampered by whistling cheerfully.

Soon Thomas came fussing. "Where's my coach?"

"Coach?" asked Donald. "What coach?"

"My special coach that Gordon brings for me. It's gone. I must find it." He bustled away.

"Gosh sakes!" said Douglas. "I might have stowed the special coach with the others."

"D'ye see that?" exclaimed Donald's Driver. A mob of angry passengers erupted from the siding. "They're complainin' to Sir Topham Hatt. He'll be comin' here next."

"Now listen," said Douglas' Driver. "We'll change tenders. Then away with ye, Donal, and take those goods. Don't worry about us. Quick now! Do as I say."

Sir Topham Hatt and three passengers walked toward them; but Donald, with Douglas' tender (10), was out and away with the goods before they came near. Douglas and his Driver waited with innocent expressions.

"Ah!" said Sir Topham Hatt, "No. 9, and why have you not taken the goods?"

"My tender is away, Sirr." The Driver showed him the tender, still uncoupled.

"I see, some defect no doubt. Tell me, why did No. 10 leave so quickly?"

"Maybe, Sirr," put in Douglas, "he saw ye comin' and thought he was late."

"Hmm," said Sir Topham Hatt.

He turned to the passengers. "Here, Gentlemen, are the facts. No. 10 has been shunting the yard. Your coach disappeared. We investigate. No. 10—er—disappears, too. You can draw your conclusions. Please accept my apologies. The matter will be investigated. Good afternoon, Gentlemen."

Sir Topham Hatt watched them till they climbed the station ramp. His shoulders twitched; he wiped his eyes. Douglas wondered if he was crying. He was not.

He swung around suddenly. "Douglas," he rapped, "why are you masquerading with Donald's tender?"

16

Now flip the book over to start another Thomas & Friends adventure.

He swung around again. "What are your names?"

"Donal an' Douggie, Sirr."

"Good!" he said. "Then your Controller can tell me which of you is which."

"Och! Ye won't get much help from him, Sirr."

"Why?"

"He doesn't know our names, Sirr. How could he? We only gave ourselves names when we lost our numbers."

"One of you," said Sir Topham Hatt, "is playing truant. I shall find him out and send him home. Inspector," he ordered, "give these engines numbers, and set them to work."

He walked sternly away.

Now flip the book over to start another Thomas & Friends adventure.

The two engines greeted him cheerfully.

"I hear you've lost your numbers," he said. "How did that happen?"

"They may have slyly slipped off Sirr. Ye know how it is." The engines spoke in chorus.

"I know. Accidentally on purpose."

The twins looked pained. "Sirr! Ye wouldn't be thinkin' we lost them on purpose?"

"I'm not so sure," said Sir Topham Hatt. "Now then, which of you is 57646?"

"That, Sirr, is just what we can't remember."

Sir Topham Hatt looked at their solemn faces. He turned away. He seemed to have difficulty with his own.

Sir Topham Hatt stared. "Did you say *two* engines, Inspector?"

"Yes, Sir."

"Then send the other one back at once."

"Certainly, Sir, but which?"

Sir Topham Hatt stared again. "Engines have numbers, Inspector," he explained patiently. "We bought No. 57646. Send the other one back."

"Quite so, Sir, but there is a difficulty."

"What *do* you mean?"

"The two engines are exactly alike, Sir, and have no numbers. They said they lost them on the way."

Sir Topham Hatt seized his hat. "We'll soon settle that nonsense," he said grimly.

"No one can say," grumbled Henry, "that we're afraid of hard work, but . . ."

" . . . we draw the line at goods trains," finished Gordon.

"Dirty freight cars, dirty sidings. Ugh!" put in James.

"What are you boiler-aching about?" asked Duck. "I remember on the Great Western . . ."

"That tin-pot railway . . ."

"Tin-pot indeed! Let me tell you . . ."

"Silence!" ordered a well-known voice. "Let me tell you that an engine for goods work will arrive from Scotland tomorrow."

The news was received with acclamation.

More and more people traveled on Sir Topham Hatt's Railway. More and more ships came to the Harbors. Everyone had to work very hard indeed.

The freight cars complained bitterly; but then, freight cars always do, and no one takes much notice.

The coaches complained, too. No sooner had they arrived with one train, than they had to go out again with fresh passengers on another.

"We don't know whether we're coming or going," they protested. "We feel *quite* distracted."

Hullo Twins!

by
The REV. W. AWDRY

SCHOLASTIC INC.

New York   Toronto   London   Auckland   Sydney
Mexico City   New Delhi   Hong Kong   Buenos Aires

Thomas the Tank Engine & Friends

A BRITT ALLCROFT COMPANY PRODUCTION

Based on The Railway Series by The Rev W Awdry
© Gullane (Thomas) LLC 2002

Visit the Thomas & Friends web site at www.thomasthetankengine.com

ISBN 0-439-33854-9

12 11 10 9 8 7 6 5 4 3 2 1   2 3 4 5 6 7/0
Printed in the U.S.A.
First Scholastic printing, August 2002

Hullo Twins!